We're Little Adventurers, one and all.
Not too little. Not too tall.

We meet each week, in our shed HQ,
ready to share our fun with YOU.

A little ADVENTURER

* IS KIND TO ANIMALS *

Even ones that don't do much
like bored worms.

* HELPS OTHERS OUT *

And not JUST for chocolate.

But we DO like chocolate AND we would share.

* IS BRAVE *

Most of the time. Sometimes things can be scary,
like things under the bed or getting soap in your eyes.

* IS HONEST AND TRUE *

In all that we do.
Hey, that rhymes!

* DOES HIS OR HER BEST *

But gets help with shoelaces
and hair washing.

* LOOKS AFTER THE PLANET *

But not all at once.
It's a very big place.

little
ADVENTURERS

LEAFY
the PET LEAF

PHILIP ARDAGH

ELISSA ELWICK

WALKER BOOKS
AND SUBSIDIARIES

LONDON • BOSTON • SYDNEY • AUCKLAND

It's time for a little adventure! Hooray!
Here are the Little Adventurers,
heading to their shed HQ.

What are they up to today?

"I've bringed my puppy!" says Finnegan.

"*Brought*," says Floss, tapping her bossy boot.

"Her name is Licky Dog," says Finnegan.

"Why's she called that then?" asks Peanut.

"*That's why*," says Finnegan.

"I've brought Pocket!" says Peanut. They go everywhere together because Pocket lives in Peanut's pocket.

"And I brought Podge," says Floss, giving her cat an extra-special squeeeeeeze.

"What pet have you brought, Sprat?" asks Finnegan.

"Shadow," says Sprat proudly, looking around for his little black cat.

Hmmmm.
Where IS Shadow?

She's not here.

She's not there.

Sprat can't see Shadow
ANYWHERE.

"I can't find Shadow," sighs Sprat.

"You have to bring in a pet. It's BRING IN A PET DAY," says Floss. "That's how it works."

Sprat really wants to join the fun.

"Maybe you could find a bug?" says Finnegan.

Going somewhere nice?

Just visiting friends.

But Sprat has a better idea.

He chooses a leaf.
Very carefully.

He chooses a crayon.
Very carefully.

He draws a face.
Very carefully.

"I've brought ... **LEAFY!**"
he says proudly.

"That'll
have to do,"
sighs Floss.

The Little Adventurers start off the day with ...

PETS' PLAYTIME!

Licky Dog catches the ball...

Podge paws at the ball.

PETS'
PLAYTIME!

SHOW
AND TELL!

WHAT MY
PET EATS!

WHEN MY PET
GROWS UP!

And Pocket sniffs at the ball.

Sprat really, really, REALLY wants to join in.

But Leafy has
his own ideas.

"Oh, Leafy!"
says Sprat.

"Podge is a CAT," says Floss. "He comes from the same family as LIONS and TIGERS!"

The Little Adventurers are VERY impressed.

"Licky Dog is just a puppy for now," says Finnegan, "but she will grow and grow and GROW!"

The others "Oooooh!"

PETS'
PLAYTIME!   SHOW
AND TELL!   WHAT MY
PET EATS!   WHEN MY PET
GROWS UP!

"I am VERY impressed," says Peanut.

Ooooh!

"Pocket is VERY good at climbing," says Peanut. "All mice are. She can climb up almost ANYTHING."

Now it's Sprat's turn.

"Leafy's favourite colour is ... **GREEN!**" he says, very pleased with himself.

WOW!

"Oh," says Peanut.

"That's nice..."
says Finnegan.

At least Snub
looks interested.

It's snack time.

WHAT MY PET EATS!

Finnegan gets to feed Floss's cat, Podge, tasty Kitty Crunch cat-treats.

CRUNCH!
CRUNCH!

Pocket eats a peanut from Peanut's pocket.

NIBBLE NIBBLE!

PETS'
PLAYTIME!
SHOW
AND TELL!
WHAT MY
PET EATS!
WHEN MY PET
GROWS UP!

Licky Dog licks
a lovely lolly.

Bad
dog!

LICK!
LICK!

But what about Leafy?

"I don't have any leaf-food for
him yet," says Sprat. "But you're
not hungry are you, Leafy?"

Leafy doesn't say ... or *do* ...
anything.

He just flutters in the breeze.

"Oh, Leafy."

Then a sudden wisp
of wind lifts the leaf
into the air.

Come back, Leafy!

WOW! Leafy is dancing!
And looping the loop!

"Look! Look!" says Sprat.

Sad Sprat sits down with a plonk, and lets Leafy have a drink of water or a swim. (Or both.)

"It's not fair. Why can't they see what a great pet you are?"

But the other Little Adventurers are far too busy to notice.

"Some cats can be ship's cats," says Floss. "Podge would make a great pet for a pirate captain."

Then – **WHOOSH!** – Leafy blows across Floss's face making ...

the perfect pirate eyepatch!

PETS'
PLAYTIME!

SHOW
AND TELL!

WHAT MY
PET EATS!

WHEN MY PET
GROWS UP!

"When Licky Dog grows up, she could be a police dog!" says Finnegan.

WHOOSH!
Look where this gust of wind lands Leafy!

"Thanks, Leafy!" says Finnegan.

"You make a great police badge!"

WANTED

"What do mice do?" Finnegan asks Peanut.

"Frighten elephants!" says Floss.

Peanut frowns. "Actually, mice are very good at singing high notes," she announces.

Pocket borrows Leafy, holding him in his tiny mouse paws.

Leafy's the perfect size to play like a teeny, tiny guitar!

It turns out that Leafy really *is* the perfect pet!

And everyone knows it.

WHOOSH!
He's off again!

"**LEAFY!**" shouts Finnegan.

Suddenly, all the Little Adventurers are laughing and racing after him.

They never guessed that chasing a leaf could be such FUN!

Back at the shed HQ, there's time for *one* extra activity ...

MAKE YOUR OWN PET LEAF!

And Sprat, Chief Leaf-Maker,
shows everyone how.

First, you choose
your leaf.

Next, you choose
your crayon.

Then, you draw
the face.

Floss draws very
carefully.

"My leaf's called
Dave!" she says.

BRING IN A PET DAY is almost over. There's just time to give out the sticky stickers.

And Sprat?

He gets the sticky sticker for being ...

THE
• little •
ADVENTURER
— WITH THE —
MOST
IMAGINATION

BRING IN A PET DAY has
been fantastic fun.

Sprat is VERY proud indeed.

"You're the best pet leaf
in the whole, wide, world,"
he whispers.

He even has a cup to prove it.

And, do you know what?
He's sure he hears Leafy give
a happy little leafy sigh.

I wonder what the
Little Adventurers will
get up to next time?

Don't you?

FLOSS's
FANTASTIC FELINE FACTS

- Feline means "to do with cats".
  I'm clever and know stuff like that.
- A group of kittens is called a kindle.

- A group of grown-up cats is called a clowder.

- Cats have five toes on each front paw but only four on each back paw.
  I checked that on Podge. It tickled him!
- Cats can jump SEVEN TIMES THEIR HEIGHT! *Imagine if we could bounce like that!*

- Cats' tongues are rough like SANDPAPER and they use them to clean and brush themselves.
  Sprat tried that with his tongue!
- Cats touch noses to say "Hello!"

PEANUT's
ALL ABOUT MICE

- A mouse's tail is as long as its body.

- Mice will sometimes play dead if they are frightened.

- A group of mice is called a mischief.

- A mouse's tail has scales to help it grip onto things when climbing.

- Mice can show other mice how they're feeling by the look on their faces. *Pocket is the best mouse in the whole wide world.*

FINNEGAN's
DOGGY FACTS

- Dogs don't have lips so they have to lap up water with their tongues.
  Licky Dog's tongue is VERY licky.

- A dog can smell ONE MILLION TIMES better than humans can.
  And Snub can out-stare Licky Dog any day.

- Dogs can hear ten times better than we can.

- Dogs do see in colour but not as well as we do.

- DOGS SHOULD NEVER EAT CHOCOLATE!
  All the more for MEEEEE!

SPRAT's
VERY IMPORTANT LEAF-AND-TREE NEWS

- Some trees keep their leaves all the year round.

- Some trees' leaves fall off in autumn. *The leaves go brown, red or yellow or gold and CRUNCHY!*

- Some trees grow up to 100 metres tall. *Which is VERY tall.*

- Some trees live for thousands of years. *So they can say "I'm older than you!" to my bossy big sister.*

- Leaves sunbathe and turn the energy of the sun into food for the trees. *I'm going to make some leafy sunglasses. I LOVE MY LEAFY!*

ARDAGH & ELWICK

Award-winning author Philip Ardagh and author/illustrator
Elissa Elwick teamed up as Ardagh & Elwick to create
the Little Adventurers. Although Ardagh writes the final
words and Elwick draws the final pictures, they work
together on making up the stories and deciding what
everyone gets up to on each page, which is far too much fun.
Ardagh is very tall with a big bushy beard. Elwick isn't.

*To all those who've had
a pet leaf, pebble, or Lego brick,
for however short a time.
P.A.*

*To Mathilda, Tom
and Sasha, for all our
little adventures. xx
E.E.*

*The Little Adventurers series is dedicated to the memory of Sally Goldsworthy
of The Discover Children's Story Centre, Stratford, East London.
She was an inspiration to so many.*

First published 2016 by
Walker Books Ltd
87 Vauxhall Walk,
London SE11 5HJ

10 9 8 7 6 5 4 3 2 1

Text and illustrations © 2016
Philip Ardagh and Elissa Elwick

The right of Philip Ardagh and
Elissa Elwick to be identified
as author and illustrator of this
work has been asserted by them
in accordance with the Copyright,
Designs and Patents Act 1988

This book has been typeset
in Century Schoolbook

Printed in China

All rights reserved. No part of
this book may be reproduced,
transmitted or stored in
an information retrieval
system in any form or by any
means, graphic, electronic
or mechanical, including
photocopying, taping and
recording, without prior written
permission from the publisher.

British Library Cataloguing in
Publication Data: a catalogue
record for this book is available
from the British Library

ISBN 978-1-4063-7399-8
(hardback)
ISBN 978-1-4063-6435-4
(paperback)

www.walker.co.uk

FSC
www.fsc.org

MIX
Paper from
responsible sources
FSC® C008047